DEAR LUCIFER AND OTHER STORIES

L.A. DAVENPORT

CONTENTS

ACKNOWLEDGMENTS

An earlier version of 'Drink, drink up, my friends' appeared in *Mind Sprocket* magazine.

Initial drafts of several of the stories were posted on *The Marching Band Emporium*, and published in a collection of the same name.

THE TEMPLE

Ben lifted his eyes and squinted at the ocean-blue sky. Sunlight baked the hard, unyielding grass and ancient carved stone. Ripples rose from the ground, swimming the nearby trees and pomegranate shrubs in a sea of relentless heat.

Ben peered at the group. The guide was still explaining what they were looking at, but Ben wasn't really listening any more.

– Temple...Greek...Doric columns...open-air altar... decorated frieze...Hera...550 BC, the guide said in his heavy Italian accent.

The air ricocheted with the clicking and sawing of insects, and Ben heard his heartbeat pounding in his ears. The material of his shirt was hot and his armpits were damp. His mouth was sticky and the dust coated his tongue.

He remembered the shop by the entrance to the archeological site and wished he had bought a bottle of water. Actually, he wished he had decided to go to the beach instead of coming on this tour. At least he could have dived into the water every now and then. Here, there was just burned grass and hot stones.

The guide, who was sensibly wearing a cap with a piece of material hanging down over his neck, started to move away, and the other members of the group, also struggling in the heat, slowly followed him. The grass crunched beneath their feet as they trudged away.

The guide's voice became lost in the rising air. Ben lifted himself from the steps of the temple, wiping the pale dust from his hands and inspecting the red indentations left by the sharp stones where he had been leaning.

– Have you been to Italy before?

Ben jumped and a headache instantly rose through his skull. He stared at a woman standing just a few feet away. He wasn't sure whether he had seen her before, but there was something familiar about her.

– Er, yes. Are you on the tour?

– No, I am in the shop.

Her accent was soft, not quite Italian. She pointed towards the entrance with a lazy arc of her arm.

– I go for walks around the site when it is quiet. It is very quiet today.

Ben looked at her again, noticing her soft dark curls, loosely tied up, and her large, dark eyes. She placed her hands on her hips and smiled. Shorts. She was wearing shorts. She had tanned, long legs and canvas trainers. And a striped t-shirt. Pretty? Handsome? No, she was much more than that. She was graceful, glowing, almost divine, despite her t-shirt and shorts.

But Ben seemed hardly able to take her in. He had spent the whole morning turning down his brain to processing only primary sensations: sharp, soft; hot, cold; bright, dark. He sighed.

– Do you like Paestum, she asked.

– Yes. It's very nice. It's a bit too warm for me today. But the temples…

He swung his arm around, looking at the ancient buildings again. No, not again; for the first time.

– The temples are really beautiful.

He smiled at her.

– Did you see the painted tombs, she asked. And the…

She frowned and looked away. – *Tuffatore*? What is the English? Yes, that's it, diver. Did you see the diver?

– Yes. He looked so real. He made me want to jump in the sea.

Ben's throat hurt as he tried to swallow.

– Do you want to swim, now? With me?

Ben frowned.

– It would be cooler, no? You are uncomfortable in the heat.

He was embarrassed and tried to hide the growing damp patches under his arms.

– We are used to it here.

She smiled and then gazed towards the rippling trees.

– I love the quiet here.

Ben listened to the insects and…nothing. He glanced over at the receding tour group. He could vaguely pick out the guide's flat drone through the rising air and the clicking and sawing of the insects. He was a little guilty. They would be finished soon, and he didn't want to appear ungrateful.

He glanced back at the woman, who was watching him with faint amusement.

– Where would we swim, he asked.

– In the sea. It's really close by, actually. It's just over there.

She smiled and pointed over the trees.

– Do you want to come?

– But, the tour…We have a bus…How would I get back?

– Don't worry, I have a car. I can drive you back to your hotel later.

Ben looked at the ancient stones, but could already the sense the cool saltwater on his skin. He smiled.

– I don't know your name.

– Some call me Angelia. And you are Ben.

She thrust out her hand, slim and tanned, with long, plain nails. Her hand was cool, almost cold to the touch. As he took her hand, something flowed through him, like electricity.

– How do you...how do you know my name?

She smiled conspiratorially and held tight onto his hand.

– I've been waiting for you.

He stared into her eyes, unable to tear away from her gaze.

– Come, let's swim.

She turned and pulled him towards the trees.

He looked back at the disappearing group in a daze. He couldn't remember, couldn't think. Now there was only the heat of the sun and the cool of the coming sea. And the electricity flowing through him from her cool hand.

He tried to focus on her shorts and tanned legs, her strong back and slim arm reaching back to him, her fingers entwined in his, unbreakably bound to him, glowing through him.

A branch hit him in the face, the leaves sharp on his skin. He closed his eyes and had a flashback to the hotel swimming pool, to the square outside the church, to the morning market, to the beach, to the shaded branches by the restaurant where he had eaten on the first night...

He opened his eyes and stared, his heart pounding. She had been in all of those places. She had everywhere, in every shadow, in every glance, in every face. She had been calling to him, waiting for him.

He stared down at her long, slim hand, unbreakably

bound in his, and then up at her strong back, as she pulled him on and on.

– Come, or the tide will go out.

THE DUST IN THE LIGHTS

– You see, I adore the applause. That's what keeps me going, really. That and the very experience of being on stage. The lights, the boards beneath my feet, the smell…You know, theatres have such a distinct smell. Something about the very particular mix of wood, varnish and plaster, I suspect, and the dust rising from the lights….

– Of course, these places have lost a lot of their character. In the old days, when Gielguid, Ralph and dear, dear Larry trod the boards, it was all so very different. Those were real actors. They made the very room come alive when they took the stage. As they emerged from the wings, you could sense a hush descend and all eyes turn to them. I tell you, it was as if the world didn't exist, except in them. Sometimes, one can almost hear their ghosts, urging one to give everything one has, to touch the audience with the unique magic of the theatre, as they so often did.

– It reminds me of when I was playing Horatio to Gielguid's Hamlet in, where was it? Guildford, I think. '55. Must have been. As I listened to him intone those marvellous words: 'Alas, poor Yorick! I knew him, Horatio; a fellow of infinite jest, of most excellent fancy,' I was transported, I tell you. I wasn't on the stage anymore. I was in a Danish grave-yard, and nothing existed but Gielguid, that skull and me. Little me, so young and so naive, really; rapt and learning at the knee of a master. 'A fellow of infinite jest.' Indeed he was. And of most excellent fancy...Everyone adored him, you know.

Malcolm gazed at the young woman sitting opposite him in his tiny, faded dressing room, the light bulbs reflecting in her glasses. She shifted nervously in her chair and smiled weakly.

– Oh, look at me, Malcolm said. Here I am wittering on about my marvellous memories of the stage. You don't want to listen to all that.

– No, it's very interesting, the young woman said hurriedly.

– You are too kind, my dear. Too, too kind. But what have you come to talk to me about? Why have you snared me here in my private lair, my refuge? I love these moments, you know, in the hours before the curtain call. Everything seems so quiet, so peaceful, while the stagehands and theatre staff flit about outside my door, getting it all ready for my appear-ance. All that for me. So kind of them. So kind.

– Well, Mr Bains.

– Do call me Malcolm, he said, patting the young woman on the knee.

– Well, Malcolm, the woman said, smiling nervously. David, your agent, asked me to come up to see you this afternoon.

– Yes, my dear?

– He asked me to come up and talk to you about the show. Unfortunately, he...he has been detained in London, so couldn't come up himself...

– That's very kind of David to send you...?

– Angela.

– Yes, Angela, thank you. It is a shame that he couldn't make it himself, after all the years we have been working together, but I am charmed to have you here, Angela.

Malcolm patted Angela on the knee again, smiling and leaning forward slightly.

– The thing is, Malcolm, David is a little worried. About the show.

– The show, my dear? I must confess that my last couple of performances have perhaps been a little flat. I have been struggling with a slight infection and I know I haven't been able to give my anecdotes about all the marvellous actors I have worked with over the years their normal zest. It may explain some of the muted responses of the audience, but I shall soon be back to my best, having them rolling in the aisles and wiping tears from their cheeks, as I have done so many times in the past.

Malcolm raised his right index finger and smiled triumphantly.

– It's nothing to do with your performances, Malcolm. They have been fine. Great, in fact.

– Indeed? What is it? Do tell.

– Well, the thing is…

– Yes?

– The things is…sales have been poor. The theatres we have done so far have been half full at best, and we're struggling to sell tickets. We have tried everything—campaigns in the local press, leaflets, posters—but the response has been… disappointing. Unfortunately, Malcolm…

– Mr Bains…

– Sorry, Mr Bains. Unfortunately, we can't sustain any more losses on the tour, and we are going to have to cancel the remaining dates.

– Including tonight?

– Yes, I'm afraid so.

Malcolm, now crumpled, looked at his wire-frame glasses, folded neatly on the dressing table, and at his make-up in its box. He hadn't started putting it on yet. No need for that now. He gazed down at his jacket and smoothed out a fold, the tweed rough under his palm.

– I am old, Malcolm said, still looking at the material of his jacket. Is that what you are telling me? I am too old?

– No, not all. It's just...

– Just what? Unpopular? No one wants to hear my stories anymore, is that it?

– I'm sorry, Mr Bains.

– I don't have anything else, you know.

– I'm so sorry.

– What am I going to do?

Malcolm looked up at Angela, tears welling in his eyes.

– I am all alone, he said. I have no one. The stage is my only friend. I have nothing else.

– I'm really sorry.

– Please. Stop saying that.

Angela looked down at the threadbare carpet as Malcolm smoothed down his jacket again.

– Shall I get you a taxi back to your hotel?

– Yes please, he said quietly.

– David told me to make sure that you got back to London okay.

– Did he? How very kind. He really should have...never mind. Angela, can I have a few moments to myself?

– Yes, of course.

– I will join you upstairs presently, but I would be alone for a little while.

DRINK, DRINK UP, MY FRIENDS

THROUGH THE HOT-FUELLED EXCESS OF A LONDON SATURDAY night comes the rising call: drink, drink up, my friends. Tonight we shall be drowned. The bitter acid taste of a glowing glass, drained to foster complicity. The swirling smear of a wooden room, a hand placed on your shoulder. You lurch your head around, blinded by the brassy bar and the smile so close to yours. There is a duty to perform, you have to be my friend tonight. Wait, you'll be back, there is another calling.

You clamber up the stairs, fighting with your unruly limbs and blocking the voices inside your head. A bawdy conversation with someone you do not know, your hand steady on cold tiles. You must wash your hands, but spill water all around. A leering glance at the ladies' queue, imagining naked flesh. Don't trip on the stairs, my friend, everyone is watching. The coldness in your cheeks, the sweat upon your brow. You are a prince tonight, your mighty mind shall fly.

Check your zip as you reach your table, throw a sloppy

grin all round. There is another glass waiting, eager eyes are on you. Time to cut a dash, employ a little bravado. Glug down your pint, even though you know it's too much. The liquid spills on your shirt, but no-one notices. Your new-found friend does not remember you, locked in conversation. So what? You can steal some time with someone new.

Up comes another rising call: one more to save our souls. Drink on, drink on. A disjointed shout goes up, others raise a hand and cheer. You look round at other tables, sorry for the tourist family. But there is no way out, you cannot cheat your new-found will. You stare at your yellow pint, watching bubbles slowly rising. Your hands have turned to lead, your eyes are becoming heavy.

That hand upon your shoulder, a different willing smile. Drink it down, my friend, show me you are one of us. I will never part from you, as long as I shall live. Open your throat just one more time; it will all soon be over. You are the last to finish, something of a failure.

They are parading out to smoke, suddenly it seems so tempting. The slamming rush into your head, it could go either way. What's that? They won't let one of us back in, one of our band of warriors. We are angry now and have to leave.

Out on the cold street, you sway and almost fall. Look back at the bouncers; they'll regret not seeing your worth. Now time for that cigarette; there's nothing when you draw. An instant headache and cold limbs, but you must smoke on. Where to now, my perfect friends forever? You cannot stop drinking now, or the hole will open up.

You fall off the curb, trying to test your balance. You notice half of them have already left; they were never really part of us. Shall we try that club? No, you have to face reality, the magic has upped and gone.

A journey on the hated bus, all jerking nausea. The stumbling walk back home, the blacked-out echoing. Climb the stairs with broken legs, pulling yourself up by your hands. Walk past the bathroom door, you mum would not approve. You crave the solace of your silken bed, the oblivion of sleep.

But your mind circles in the street-lit room, there is no rest tonight.

HAVE YOU SEEN AN ANGEL?

– Do you notice anything different about me?

– No.

He stared back at me, searching my face. Perhaps there is, I thought, but I didn't want to say so.

– I saw an angel, he said quietly. It was when I was in the park the other day. At least that's what I think I saw. Whatever it was, it glowed with a bright, golden light as it came down from the sky. When it got closer, I could see its wings beating, in time to a heavenly melody. The music filled the air and silenced the noises of the city.

He glanced down at the Formica-topped table, and picked at a small nick in the brown and white surface.

– You don't believe me, do you?

He started straight up at me, his eyes steady, but his voice trembling. There was a lifetime in his stare. A cascade of hope and ambitions, illusions and failures.

I didn't know what to say.

– Sometimes, you know, even I'm not sure of what I saw. I suppose it could have been a hallucination, or maybe a ghost. Maybe I'll never know. But it seemed so real, you know? When it happened, everything disappeared. I couldn't hear the children and dogs playing, and the traffic passing on the road. I was completely absorbed by the flowing, golden light.

Eventually, he stopped talking. He finished off his cold coffee in one swift gulp and asked me whether I wanted another. I shook my head.

We have known each other forever, but now I don't know what to say to a man I no longer recognise; a man who is struggling with something neither of us can understand.

I would like to leave this dead-end cafe, to sneak out of the back while he pays at the till. But I know I could never escape his having told me, even if I managed to get away from him.

At the till his hand shakes as he counts out a few coins. He is a broken shadow of himself, a shattered soul. But who can judge a man who believes in something? Haven't we all wished that we could have seen an angel through the nagging darkness that surrounds us?

He returns to the table with a nervous smile, sliding into the anonymous seat with palpable relief, away from the stares of people who do not know his turmoil. There is hope, doubt, pain and delight in his eyes. He searches mine for a strand of understanding and shared insight. I smile back at him, trying to be convinced.

THE LAST MOMENT

I SOMETIMES IMAGINE YOUR LAST MOMENT; THAT LONELY death-roll of metal and glass in a country lane.

When the ambulance took you, I was reading the recipe.

When you sank away from me, I was laying out the plates.

As I wondered if you had forgotten, the telephone rang.

THE VISIT

– Come in, sit down and have a cup of tea. Give me a kiss on my powdered, wrinkled skin. Hold your breath as the musty smell of my clothes fills your nose, and smile awkwardly as I move away from your cheek.

– Nod at the pictures I point out on the mantelpiece and make all the right noises as I tell you about my worsening health. Stroke the cat's head as she hisses at you on her way past. Peer through the net curtains obscuring your view and say how nice the garden is looking. Go to the loo for far too long, and stare at your watch, wondering how long you should stay.

– Stroke the arm of the chair, with its doily to stop the dirt getting in. Look at your shoes as I tell you about half-forgotten memories of long ago, when Churchill was in power and you could still get change from a pound for a day out on the train. Look at my hands, wrinkled and puffy, as I fiddle with the catch on a box of old postcards.

– Stare at my thin, wispy hair and my old-fashioned make-up. Eat one more biscuit, as I force the niceties of a forgotten era down your throat. Watch the time tick by slowly and invent a train you have to catch, an appointment you have to keep. Smile weakly at my advice and think me naive, in your conviction of how things should be done.

– Talk about things you no longer care about, and become embarrassed as I remind you of your youthful days. Become impatient and bored, and start ignoring me, pacing up and down the room, fingering objects you barely noticed before. Decide finally to leave, raising your voice over my trailing conversation.

– Only then will I decide to say something interesting. But it will be too late, you will have started to leave. Your carefully developed excuse will leave you no imaginary time to fit in just five more minutes, to enjoy the glint in my watery eyes, the laugh hidden in the creases around my mouth, unnoticed until now.

– Realise that I am more than just a weekly duty you perform to prop up your conscience. See that there is more to me than you have thought to imagine. Observe that my world was more than the deteriorating remains of a family home, tentative trips to the grocers and shuffling to the Post Office every week.

– Notice that I am what you will become, that I am your future. But lie more to cover up your lie. Leave my house with a lingering sense of guilt that makes you hate yourself as you hurriedly smoke a cigarette on the graffitied platform of the station.

– Promise yourself that, next week, you will appreciate me more, that you will not spend your time thinking about drunkenness, sex and office gossip. But forget that vow the next time you look at your watch and realise that you are late in coming to see me.

WAITING

You arrive early.

The bar fills; you look down as people glance your way.

People ask to take the other chair.

An hour passes; finally you agree.

After a while, you stop drinking, worried that you are becoming drunk.

He will come, you tell yourself. This time, he will come.

DEAR LUCIFER

To his Satanic Majesty, Lucifer, the Fallen Angel,

My Lord,

I do hope you forgive the impertinence of writing to you directly, but I'm afraid I cannot think of any other way of reaching you. I have already tried a séance and endured a frankly disappointing evening with a Ouija board. There was even one rather unfortunate episode when I attempted to sacrifice an animal, but it did not go quite as planned. At least I now know that I enjoy curried goat.

The thing is, I am at my wits end and I therefore thought it might be an idea to write you this letter. In short, I would like to ask you if we could meet, should you have a few moments to spare. You see, I have a few problems that I would like to discuss with you face-to-face, and perhaps ask your advice. I might even like to ask your assistance, if that would not be too presumptuous.

The main difficulty with contacting you is that I am not sure of the protocol. Do you take appointments, or are things not so organised? Do you have a secretary, or maybe a PA? Is there somewhere I can visit you at your work, or do you come to me? Should I reserve an office? Order tea and biscuits? Maybe a flip chart and a set of pens? I did wonder if you would prefer something to be included with this letter, as a small gift and statement of intent? I thought perhaps of including some drops of blood, or an old skull? However, I feared you would find all that a bit old fashioned.

Besides, I am sure you are very busy, with so much on your plate. All those endless problems and cases to solve. Although I imagine it cannot be easy encouraging evil these days. After all, how you judge something evil depends on how you define morality and goodness, and with things so… relative nowadays, it is not so easy to be sure of what is right and wrong.

Or am I simply missing the point? Is the reason we have not heard from you for so long that your work is done? Are we no longer worth the effort of convincing us to be evil? Have we already fallen so far from goodness that you have simply hung up your tarnished wings and settled into a comfortable retirement? After all, who can be diverted from the chosen path when the path we have chosen is so strewn with sin and excess?

When I think about it, if we have already fallen into the hellfire, that leaves you in the difficult position of encouraging us to be better, if our humble lives are to be undone. In the end, evil can have no meaning if it does not come from goodness.

However, I will importune you with my ramblings no longer; rather, I would much prefer to talk in person. You see, I would like to do so many bad and reprehensible things; I would like to commit evils and ruin lives. But I am unfortunately wracked with guilt at my desires and the harm that they could do; so much so, that it stops me in my tracks before I can get beyond the planning stage. Perhaps you could help me to overcome my reticence and convince me of the necessity of evil, and that I need not worry about my conscience?

Of course, nothing is given without something in return. I have heard from reliable sources that you might be happy to take my soul, if that would be of interest. I certainly do not plan on making use of it for much longer.

Until such time as we can meet, I remain at your disposal.

My Lord,

Your lordship's most humble,

most obedient servant

GOING THROUGH THE MOTIONS

ELEANOR STOPPED AND PUSHED BACK HER HAIR, BLOWN forward in the cold, hard wind. What was she doing? She was supposed to be at the gallery by now to meet...what was he? A friend? A date? She thought back to the party in Clapham the previous weekend. She had been drunk, but not that drunk, and he was nice enough. All smiles and attentiveness. He had laughed at her jokes and seemed interested in her work and what she had to say.

And she was interested in him. Or at least she wasn't uninterested. Plus, he wasn't unattractive. Perhaps a little short for her. But, then, most men were. And he worked in publishing, which was pretty much the same as everyone else she knew.

What was it that made her want to see him again? Was she going through the motions? Did she think she needed someone, anyone, and he would do? Is that all it was? Shouldn't she be waiting for the hit, the buzz, the gut-tugging pull of excitement that told her this could be forever, even after such a short time? Or was a certain sense of emptiness a sign of something more practical and, in the end, more fulfilling?

Maybe I shouldn't question it so much, she thought. She gazed down at the cracks in the pavement and the dots of chewing gum ageing into black holes and then checked her watch. She was going to be late to meet him, but she didn't really care. That meant something, surely.

People started pushing past her, so she walked to the riverside and looked over the edge. The tide was out and the grey-brown mud exposed. A few gulls were searching for food and staring at the glistening water. What were they looking at? She gazed at the swell and the tiny waves whipped up by the gentle afternoon breeze. She couldn't see anything.

On the opposite bank, cars and people moved silently. All those lives that she could never know, she mused. Some must be tourists, some on their way to work. Maybe some are driving to a weekend away, a dinner party, a wedding, a funeral. How many were setting out on a journey into the unknown? How many thought they were in stasis, just going through the motions? Was she the only one? Or are we all the same: bored automatons listlessly doing the next thing because that's what comes next?

She stopped looking at the people, the cars, the water, the gulls. She stopped listening to the half-snatched conversations of passers-by, to the lapping of the water, the squawking of the birds, the engines of the riverboats, and the distant roar of the city that had her surrounded.

But she couldn't stop listening to the nagging, troubled doubts in her mind. She was claustrophobic. There was nowhere to go. She could turn around and walk away, but to what? Back to her flat? Back to the tedious flatmates and the possessions that she knew all too well? She could watch a film, get a train. Pointless, all. And what of that poor soul waiting outside the gallery? Surely he was checking his watch by now, searching the milling faces for someone he recognised, wondering if he had forgotten what she looked like, wondering if he should call her. It was all so predictable.

A noise broke into her mind. It was a shout, from someone close by. She turned to see a woman pointing desperately at the bridge. Eleanor studied the painted iron arches. What was it? She couldn't spot anything. And then she saw it. A man had clambered over the side of the bridge and was stepping from giant rivet to giant rivet, trying to pick his spot. He was dressed in a loose t-shirt and a pair of combat trousers, but no shoes. She could see his hair, blown by the breeze. He looked cold, or scared. But he was certainly determined. Eventually, he reached the middle of an arch. He turned his back to the metalwork and faced the river, the city, the sky.

More people had noticed him. Some were calling out, while others panicked, wondering what to do, or made phone calls. One man, a tourist, was filming it all with his phone. Faint sirens were in the distance, but they could have been for anything. All the while, Eleanor stood motionless, transfixed. The moment seemed to last forever.

Then there was a faint push, a contraction of the shoulders. The man arched his back and swung his arms above his head, like an Olympic diver, and everyone watching fell silent as he sprung off the metal arch. He looked graceful, bird-like, even, swooping down to pluck a fish from the watery depths. A woman shouted.

– Nooo…

Of course it was too late. It had been too late ever since he contracted his shoulders. And down he fell, faster and faster, towards the grey concrete river. At the last moment, he changed his position, and landed flatly, heavily on the surface, and fought against the engulfing waves.

But there was nothing he could do. The current was pulling him under, pulling him under the bridge and down into the blackness. In a second, he was gone. Eleanor looked down and, not knowing what to do, stared at her fingernails. The red varnish she had painted on the week before was chipped and missing in places. She didn't know what to think. She wanted to cry, but not for him. People were walking past. For them, nothing had happened.

She started running, towards where the man had jumped, but she carried on, far beyond, pushing through the crowd with an increasing sense of panic. She was heading towards the gallery, to the man she had met the previous Sunday, but she knew that was not where she was going. She wanted to run forever and be swept up by the wind and disappear. She ran on and on, hardly noticing where she was going.

Eventually, she stopped near London Bridge, almost collapsing with exhaustion and cursing her unfit body. She looked around. Everything looked different. Something had changed. No, not something. It was her; she had changed.

She was alive, burning with fear and awake to her every thought and sensation. She searched the faces of the passers-by, still breathing heavily. They didn't know, they couldn't see it. But she knew. She knew she had to hold onto that, to that fear and that wakefulness, if she was going to stop going through the motions and not end up push herself off into a grey concrete oblivion.

She looked around, and started running again.

THIS IS IT

SUNLIGHT BURST THROW THE DIRTY METAL-FRAMED WINDOW and illuminated the plain coffee table that stood in the middle of the room. A young man lay sprawled on a beige sofa, pock-marked with cigarette burns. He stared absent-mindedly at a small television that sat squat on the floor in a corner.

– Join us after the break, when we will be talking to a put-upon mother and her drug-addict prostitute of a daughter, the host announced, wearing a carefully rehearsed expression of concerned disgust. The audience booed and then clapped.

The young man gazed at the blank walls of the room and then back at the television.

– Have you got debts that leave you with a headache at the end of every month? Do you find it hard to keep up with all the different payments you have to make? With one of our special loans, you can consolidate all of your debts into one, easy payment that will leave you enough money left over so you can enjoy a new lease of life...

A thought tried to force its way into the young man's

mind, but gave up and sank back into oblivion. Something about debts, maybe something about drugs. He considered changing the channel, but he couldn't summon up enough energy to reach for the remote control, which lay a few inches from his hand.

Hungry? Nope. In any case, I can't be bothered to go to the kitchen. What's there? A couple of slices of bread and a half-eaten pizza. No butter for the bread. No plates, just one dirty knife. And I can't be bothered to clean it.

Applause.

– Welcome back. Now, Jessie is a hard-working single mum, making ends meet with a job at a call centre and spending all her spare cash on making sure that her daughter, Nikkala, has all she needs. She sacrifices everything for her daughter, and hasn't been out for a drink with a friends for months.

– Aaah, intoned the audiences.

– And, she hasn't been on holiday for, well…let's find out. Can we bring out Jessie? Let's get her out.

Applause.

An overweight, depressed-looking woman wearing a tracksuit wandered out onto the stage.

– Welcome to the show Jessie.

More applause.

– Take a seat. Thanks for joining us, Jessie.

– That's all right, Jessie said, making herself comfortable in one of two armchairs at the front of the stage.

– Okay, so when was the last time you went on...

Click. Silence.

The remote control bounced on the sofa and landed on the laminate floor, the cover opening on impact and scattering two batteries. The young man listened to the echo resonating around the room, and then the silence. There was nothing, not even a bird singing outside. Just the faint whirring of a truck far, far below and the distant rumble of the city.

He glanced at the blank walls and then back at the blank television before slowly pulling himself off the sofa. He thought about having a shower, but couldn't be bothered.

A quick check in the mirror. Yep, hair looks okay.

He pulled up his t-shirt and looked at his sunken stomach, the hunger growling within. Soon sort that out, he said to himself, pulling on a pair of battered trainers and reaching for his key on the floor by the door.

Soon he was riding down in the urine-stinking lift, watching the numbers change rhythmically. When they reached 10, the doors opened with a rattle and he trudged along the walkway, not bothering to look out at the ragged mass of south London, not registering the sharp wind tugging at his t-shirt and pushing onto his skin, not noticing the puddles on the bare concrete.

Number 1042.

He stood at the door and thought about what he would find inside. He was a little nervous. It was only a few hours since he had sunk into blissful emptiness, letting all thoughts and concerns slip away, drifting into calm stasis, but it could have been the first time again. He thought back to the clear, simple days when he didn't go to the flat, when it all seemed so exciting.

It wasn't exciting now. It was necessity, and he knew he shouldn't be there. But he feared more what lay in wait if he didn't go, and so pressed the bell with steady determination. He pulled himself together, gathering his will to force himself on.

A noise from within and a couple of footsteps. A bolt shot back and the frame creaking slightly as the dirty, peeling door began to open. This is it. His heart pounded. This is it.

RESPECT FOR THE DEAD

THE DARK HORSE SHAKES ITS HEAD SLOWLY, SENDING THE JET-black plumes in its harness into a syncopated dance. Another, shackled alongside and looking into the distance, waits silently, shining in the bright sunshine. A small crowd of people, all dressed in black, breaks and gets into a line of waiting cars. After grinding a cigarette into the grey tarmac and waiting for a white van to pass, the coachman straightens his black top hat and climbs onto the box of the hearse. He adjusts his tailcoat and takes up the reins.

Slowly, the hearse creeps forward, the horses repeatedly bowing their heads and rattling their harnesses as they take their first steps. The metal-rimmed wheels of the hearse clatter on the stone-encrusted road, and the flowers shiver in the wreath on the top of the hearse. One by one, the cars judder into life and the solemn procession inches along the street. No need to hurry. Not now.

An old man, walking home with plastic bags full of shopping, stops and doffs his cloth cap. A cat, folded under a heavy bush, watches the horses pass and a dog barks, intoxicated on the equine sweat drifting in the half-breeze.

In the leading car, a woman, trying not to cry, looks away from her husband and out of the window, not noticing the crumbling tower block and the anonymous houses staring back at her. A group of children stop playing and even the greasy pigeons, swooping for a discarded burger, suspend their fight for survival to honour a battle recently lost. Only an empty crisp packet, circling on the pavement in a dust tornado, ignores the procession.

As the hearse reaches the junction, cars slow and conversations abruptly end. Faces turn to see the horses and the shaking plumes.

– I didn't know they still did things like that here, someone says. I thought it was just in the East End.

– Nice, though, isn't it? A bit of respect for the dead. Know what I mean?

A Turkish man, placing melons into a crate outside his shop, straightens and watches, puzzled. The procession passes in front of the Co-op and the print shop. A drunk emerges from the pub and stops, bowing his head clumsily.

You are leaving the Post Office, thinking of nothing, putting your wallet away. It's the clip-clop of shod hooves that catches your attention. And a women by the bus stop making the sign of the cross. You want to take a picture when you see the incongruous majesty of it all, but a cloud passes in front of the sun and you are cold and uncomfortable, shuddering slightly.

Who is that in the wooden box with the brass handles? No one you know. You think of your mother. She is still alive, but you will be in a car with blacked-out windows soon enough.

A motorbike passes, loud and fast, and the horses stop, panicked. The coachman sways on his box and gathers himself, gently flicking the reins.

– No bloody respect, a voice says. That's the trouble with people today.

The old man curls his face and spits in disgust. The hearse moves forward again, up the hill towards the white-painted prison and another world. As the last of the black cars passes, you wake, as if from a dream. You want to talk to someone, to those standing around, but you realise you don't know anyone. These people, this...community; it's not your home, even though you live here.

Slowly, the noise builds and the faces turn away.

DAY AND NIGHT

Day
Dogs on leads
Tight-stretched t-shirts
Sun-dappled taxis
Wind-blown trees
Drifting clouds
Striding suits
Tourist walks
Glinting domes
Running shoes
Swept-back hair
Clacking heels
Shaded prams
Happy faces
Downcast eyes
Laughing children
Chatting mothers
Roaring lorries
Whining scooters
Thudding jacks

Rumbling trains
Sweet wrappers
Forgotten coffees
Rolling coins
Chasing hands
Pecking pigeons
Stealthy cats
Yellow workmen
Tilted dustcarts
Shop front windows
Stuck-on posters
Wailing sirens
Mobile phones

Night
Clattering trains
Lolling drunks
Snapping cameras
Hoarse songs
Thudding bars
Yellow street lamps
Roaring buses
Falling shadows
Laughing mouths
Flash-point shouts
Crying eyes
Stumbling feet
Short-cut dresses
Battered pumps
Crushed chips
Scattered bones
Earnest faces
Flying arms
Empty cartons

Spilled drinks
Fizzing lager
Bored barmen
Pushing shoulders
Flashed tattoos
Cabaret smut
Plucked eyebrows
Scanning glances
Undone ties
Electro beats
Shuffling wallflowers
Intense embraces
Lost exchanges

And me, alone
Forever walking
Avoiding glances
Watching all

I WILL DO ANYTHING

THE TALL, WELL-DRESSED MAN SLOWLY PULLED ASIDE THE curtain, the thick, heavy material tugging as the wooden rings caught against the rail. Inside, the room was dark, and the smell of stale, damp air, mixed with human sweat, attacked his nose as he entered.

It had taken him an hour to find the house in the forgotten back streets of the city, and the initial relief at reaching his destination was soon replaced with a dread sense of unease when he had knocked on the wooden door and it swung open of its own accord. The house was silent, save a series of unearthly groans coming from the first floor, and he became aware of his footsteps as he walked carefully across the bare, dirty boards.

Twice he called out before a small, thin voice from somewhere within the bowels of the house replied. There was no light, save for a patch of winter sunshine that illuminated the hallway from the open door, and it took him several minutes to identify the source of the voice.

He wasn't aware of how long he had waited in front of the filthy curtain before he had dared to draw it back, but now he stood, adjusting his eyes to the blackness and trying to revive the compulsion that had driven him to seek out this woman from another world.

– Come in.

The man jumped, but quickly gathered his composure. The voice had come from somewhere over to his left, but he could see only vague shapes.

– Don't worry. There's no need to be afraid. Let the curtain drop and I will light a candle.

The man did as she said. He heard a match strike, and caught sight of a thin, bony hand in the yellow glow. The wick took several seconds to catch, during which the man wondered whether he should run, back to the safety of own his house, his life. But he stood firm, willing himself not to shiver.

Once the candle had lit, he could see the face of an old woman sitting hunched in a threadbare armchair between a dirty stove and a small day bed. The woman was dressed in what appeared to be a pile of rags, and her greasy, straggly hair stuck out an angles from beneath an old bonnet.

Aside from the bed and stove, the room was sparsely furnished, with just a single chair in the middle and a battered trunk pushed into a corner. On the wall above the bed was a smoke-stained picture of a street scene, while the wall opposite had been daubed with a series of strange markings drawn in what appeared to be brown ink, although it struck the man with a shudder that it could just as easily be dried blood.

– Why don't you sit down?

The woman motioned to the chair and the man perched himself on the edge of the seat, trying not to get his clothes dirty.

– You have come a long way to find me, particularly as

you chose to walk all the way. Why didn't you bring your carriage?

– I didn't want anyone to know I was coming.

– I thought so. She nodded her head slowly. – Is that because the idea made you uncomfortable, or because you didn't want to get your wife's hopes up, in case I failed to help her.

– How did you know…?

The woman waved her hand dismissively.

– I make it my business to know. You would be surprised what an old woman who never leaves her room can find out about a gentleman, especially an old woman with friends like mine.

She laughed and shook her head.

– Yes, I can find out a lot, my friend, and you couldn't imagine what sort of clues law-abiding, morally upstanding people like you leave lying around. When you have nothing to hide, there's nothing you can hide, you know.

The man stared at the floor. After a while, he looked back up at the old woman and frowned.

– So you know why I am here?

– Yes, after a fashion, but I would prefer it if you told me the story yourself.

The man looked around the room again and cleared his throat.

– Well, a few months ago, my wife became ill.

– Yes?

– Very ill, as a matter of fact. We took her to see several doctors, each of whom told us a different story.

– Pah! Doctors.

The man sighed and looked down at the floor.

– One said she had pleurisy, another consumption, another a derangement of her circulation, and yet another said she was merely hysterical. In each case, the doctor wrote out a prescription for ever-more expensive medications, none of which made her any better. As a matter of fact, most of them made her worse. One doctor even suggested blood-letting, which made her so faint that I thought she might die.

The old woman inclined her head.

– Very upsetting, I'm sure.

– Yes, it was. My wife was distraught, and I don't mind saying that I was at my wit's end.

– Indeed, the woman said gently.

– Eventually, I decided that enough was enough. I withdrew a substantial portion of my savings and took her to see the Queen's Physician. At first, he didn't want to see us, but an acquaintance of mine put in a good word for me and I secured an appointment. After a thorough examination of my wife and a lengthy consultation, he told me that my wife had a cancer of the lung, he believes resulting from an injury she sustained when she slipped on the ice last winter. Not only that, but he said that he had no treatment for her, and that she had only a few months to live. That was two months ago, and she is fading away day by day.

– Terrible, terrible, the woman said, shifting in her armchair.

The man fell silent, trying to gather his thoughts and fight back the tears.

– And now you have come to see me in the hope that I can in some way help your wife?

The man lifted his head.

– Yes.

– There are a few possibilities that come to mind, and you are certainly not the first gentleman I have had in my chamber asking for help in such matters. However, there are several considerations we must address before we get to that point. While I shan't be as expensive as the Queen's Physician, I will, of course, incur certain…expenses.

– I understand. I am not without money.

– Good. The old woman frowned and pointed a finger at the man. And you must do exactly as I say, no matter how strange or outlandish it seems. You must understand that, without following my instructions to the letter, it will be impossible for me to help your wife, and she will die.

The old woman's eyes seemed to glow in the half-light, trapping the man in their gaze.

– Anything. I will do anything.

DO YOU WANT TO STAY?

AFTER A WHILE, HE STOPPED COUNTING THE LIGHTS. THERE were too many of them and, anyway, it was getting cold. So they sat there in silence, staring down over the town from their bench at the top of the park.

– Where's your house, then?

A slim finger pointed across the valley. The boy tried to follow the line, but it was no use. He couldn't work out which light he was pointing at.

– Where? I can't see.

The finger pointed harder, more insistently.

– There.

The boy looked again, but it was impossible.

– Oh yes, he lied. – I see.

They fell into silence again.

– Have you been before?

– Where, the park?

– No, to see your family.

– Oh, no. I haven't. I didn't even know I had family before they wrote. I thought I was an orphan.

– Do you like this lot, then? Your proper family, I mean.

– I don't know. They seem all right. Why?

– Just wondered. I've wondered sometimes…you know, what it'd be like if a different family turned up and took me away.

– Really? Have you?

– Sometimes.

A wind whipped across the top of the valley. One of the boys yawned and shivered.

– I suppose we'd better go back.

– I suppose so.

Neither boy moved.

– Are you scared?

– A bit.

– Of what?

– That my real family will make me stay here.

– Don't you like it here?

– No, it's not that. It's nice here. But…

– But what?

The boy swallowed and looked out over the lights and the dark valley spread out before them.

– It's just that I love my step-family. They're like my real family. I'm scared I won't see them again.

– Don't worry, no one can make you do something you don't want to.

– No, I suppose not. Can we stay friends, even if I don't stay here?

– 'Course.

– Thanks.

MANHOLE

Hello. Can you help me? I seem to have got myself stuck. Sorry to be a bore. I know you must be terribly busy, but if you could just spare a moment...No? Of course not, I understand. Maybe someone else might...Ah, yes, hello? No? Maybe you...Hello? You, over there...Sorry to bother you. I wouldn't normally ask but...It's all a bit embarrassing, I know, but I was wondering...No? Oh well, never mind. Excuse me. Sir? No? Not at all. I do realise this is a bit of an imposition. Hello? How about you? No? Oh well, I'm sure I'll be fine. I'll just wait here until someone...Funny, really. I mean, me ending up stuck in this, well, manhole. Stuck, you know. A man, in a hole...A man in a manhole...It's just that, in case anyone does fancy...I mean, if they have the time, as it were...Just a tug should do it. A quick pull on my hands. Wouldn't take a moment. And then I'd be out in a jiffy... Gosh, everyone is so busy this morning. Ow. No, sorry. My fault. I shouldn't be stuck down this hole, then you wouldn't end up having to kick me in the back on your way to work. My, it is busy, isn't it? Lots of people...Ow. Yes, sorry, I know. I shouldn't have got so drunk. It's my fault for getting married, of course. Those fellows, they had to do something to mark the occasion. Mind you, I think even they excelled themselves with this particular wheeze. What was that? No, madam, I am not mad. Just talking out loud to whoever will listen, as it were. In actual fact, I'm trying to attract some attention, maybe even convince someone to give me a hand. You know, a quick tug. No, I can assure you that it wasn't my intention to find myself stuck halfway down a manhole in the pavement right outside Victoria Station at eight on a Monday morning. Yes, I realise that it is an inconvenience to you, but believe you me, the inconvenience to me is far gr...No, no, just overweight, madam. I prefer overweight, if you don't mind. No, my feet aren't resting on anything, just dangling, thank you for asking. Yes, that's right. I am completely stuck. It's rather an odd sensation, if I may say. Like floating, I imagine, although I have never been much of a swimmer...Ah, yes. Would you excuse me, madam? I would like to attract the attention of...Good morning, kind sir, I could indeed do with a hand. Maybe a quick tug...No? You just fancied a laugh at my expense? I see. Well, who can blame you? I am sure I would have done the same. Ow...Yes, another kick in the back. Very sharp shoes you have there, sir. They could serve you well in some sort of combat situa-tion...Ah, wonderful, a group of Japanese tourists. Just what I need. Do I mind? What? You taking your photograph with me? No, not at all. Go right ahead. I think you're going to have to crouch down, if we are both going to get in the picture...You want me to smile? Right. Well, there we go. What was that? A typical English ritual? I suppose so. In some ways. Is it traditional for a man who is getting married...? Yes, yes, that's right. They were indeed playing a trick on the groom. I suppose it was very funny, unless you happen...No, I was hoping to get out before now. Ever since I woke up this morning at 5am to the sound of the pavements being cleaned. No, no one has helped me in all that time. It is extraordinary, isn't it? Actually, pretty much everyone has ignored me. And there have been a few laughs at my expense, I can tell you. No, you were the first who wanted to take my picture...Is that a policeman? No, just over there, near the public telephones. Could you attract his attention, please? No? You've got to get a taxi? Of course you have, but it wouldn't take a moment to call him...You're in a hurry? Of course you are. And what is five more minutes to me, after all, seeing as I've been down here for so long? Don't worry, he's spotted me. I can see him coming over now, in fact...Ah, good morning officer. How are you today? Yes, indeed, as you say: In better shape than me. I dare say. Well, to be honest, you are not going to believe what happened to me...

THE ELECTRIC LOVE STORY

THE MOST EXCITING BAND TO HAVE COME OUT OF LONDON SINCE that belt factory closed down, Electric Love took the world by storm when they released their international smash-sensation debut album five years ago. Made up of teenage heartbreaker hi-lo and LA Dave, the mercurial producer who pioneered the legendary 'vintage jam' technique, Electric Love rewrote the rule book of what pop, art, pop-art, art-pop and pop-pop could be. Now, in the definitive account of their meteoric rise to fame and their equally rapid fall from grace, Bob Caramel *gets to the heart of the band and tells their story in three separate interviews that reveal the highs and lows of life in the spotlight.*

IT WAS A BEAUTIFUL DAY. Sunny. Hardly a cloud in the sky. The sort of day on which you could fall in love, see a film, roll around in the park, buy a milkshake, help an old lady across the road, fall out of love, drop a Magnum into the gutter, find a fiver in your pocket, lose it all on the slots, open a bank account and still have time for dinner with your mates. No one would argue with that. Not even them. Mind you, if they did, they were the kind of people you would instantly believe. And make you wish it would start raining.

They? Oh, 'they' are hi-lo and LA Dave. And 'they', together, form Electric Love, the electro-smash-bubble-pop-sensation that took the world by storm and never let it go.

I first met them years ago, right at the start of their incredible journey. It was a cold Sunday afternoon in late April, and they were playing a gig in a tiny pub behind the old Magnet bar in Soho. She was sporting a bleach-blond asymmetrical haircut and was dressed in a gold mini dress and shocking pink leggings that had all the heads turning. He was dressed in a baggy shirt, old denim jacket and chinos. Neither of them are dressed that way today. They wouldn't. They couldn't. Too much has happened. And that's what they are here to tell me about.

It takes them five minutes to climb the stairs to the small office overlooking Brixton High Street. It isn't my office. I later find out it isn't their office. Further enquiries reveal it isn't anyone's office. They, hi-lo and LA Dave, Electric Love, had seen it on the internet and rented it out for the day. For the day of the interview. That's the kind of people they are.

As they climb the stairs, they're talking. I can hear them. They sound pleased to see each other. It sounds like months since they last met.

– Is it months since you last met, I ask them as they walk into the room and look around, taking it all in.

She, hi-lo, is dressed in a yellow bomber jacket, distressed Japanese anime t-shirt and low-slung skintight jeans. Her shoes look as if they have been spliced with a pair of trainers. I later find out they have. Literally. He, LA Dave, is wearing nothing. Nothing at all. Apart from white t-shirt that looks like it's shrunk in the wash, frayed combat trousers and a pair of slip-on tasselled loafers.

LA Dave looks at hi-lo. hi-lo looks back at LA Dave. They

both laugh. Out loud. They look at me. I laugh, although I don't know why.

LA Dave. He could still be the same naive, trusting, wide-eyed teenager I met all those years ago, apart from the crow's feet and the paunch. And the oddly grey hair. And her? hi-lo? She doesn't look a day older than that smile she gave me back then, when I asked her about her legion of adoring males fans, me included. That smile. It's 1,134 days old. She looks 1,134 days older. Maybe more. But they still look like they could fill the dance floor at the flick of a greasy chord.

– It's been six weeks, LA Dave says.

– What has, I ask, puzzled.

– Since we last met.

– Who, I ask. I had almost forgotten my question.

LA Dave looks at hi-lo and laughs. They both laugh. I laugh. I still don't know why.

But they aren't here to talk about any of that. hi-lo and LA Dave, Electric Love, are here to talk about themselves, their music, the highs, the lows, the in-betweens, the rights, the lefts and the just-over-theres.

It all started so simply. He was a struggling producer; she was a singer with a string of underground hits to her name. The trouble was, they were all so underground that no-one outside her immediate family had heard them.

But all that was about to change.

One cold January morning on a February evening in March, LA Dave, drunk and stumbling around after another failed project, walked around a corner, a corner that happened to be just around the corner from the office in which we are currently sitting, and walked straight into a bleached blonde ingénue. Actually, he tripped over his shoe laces and fell at her feet.

– Yeah, I remember that! LA Dave thumps the table and stares at hi-lo.

– She cuts in: Yeah, LA kinda lay there for a minute, like he was, like, dead or something. It was, like, totally cube and I laughed, yeah?

– LA Dave laughs too and looks back at me, adding: I was totally oblivious of everything. Even my hair. I was that macked.

– hi-lo: Yeah, you totally were. You were drunk. It was well cube. And then, right there, he vomited. On the floor, in front of my plats. I laughed. I said to him: man, this must be, like, love.

– LA Dave takes up the story: I looked up. And there, right above me, was this, like, sign. It said 'Electric Avenue'. And she looked down at me, yeah? I was still totally macked-out on the floor, and I said: Hey, it must be Electric Love. And right there and then, I knew we had something.

And so it proved. Over the next six months, they spent literally hours in the studio, perfecting soon-to-be-legendary dancefloor killer faves such as: 'Bounce (Bounce)', 'Push The Door (Open)', 'Ashtray (On My Windowsill)', 'Can You Hand Me (A Pen)'; 'Will I Be In The Movies? (I Suspect Not)', and 'Do You Want (A Cup Of Tea)', all of which formed the core of their groundsealing debut album, Can I Have That (Please?).

– What inspired the name, I ask hi-lo.

She looks nervously at LA Dave and then confidently back at me.

– What name, she asks.

– The name of your album, I say.

hi-lo frowns, then laughs.

– I, like, said, 'Can I have that, please?' a lot when I asked him for things. LA thought it was kinda sweet, so we used it.

– And what, I ask, inspired the sound, that electro-bubble-pop-gum sound that was so much a part of your identity?

LA Dave looks at the floor and knits his fingers.

– I like chewing gum, sometimes. I like fish fingers and baked beans, sometimes. I like *Heat* magazine, chick flicks and action movies. Sometimes. Sometimes I don't. Sometimes I like olives, delicately spiced Moroccan food and the work of Kieślowski. Sometimes. But sometimes I don't.

LA Dave pushes his sunglasses up his nose and looks out of the window. I see a bus reflected in the curves of his lenses. I think it's the 159 to Streatham. That bus goes up the hill. But it isn't over the hill. Yet.

THE NEXT TIME I see hi-lo and LA Dave we are in Shoreditch. Well, Hoxton, but you know what I mean. In a tiny place off Hoxton Square. I'd better not say the name of the impossibly trendy bar where we met or it will stop being impossibly trendy and just become trendy. Or worse.

Everyone in there is ultra-bosh, as they would call it, if they aren't too flip-out trendy to use such words. Almost too ultra-bosh, if that's even possible. If it is possible, 'too ultra-bosh' would happen there. Right there. Maybe nowhere else.

Let me give you an example.

While I'm waiting for them, hi-lo and LA Dave, I see a young kid pop out. He is wearing a sky-blue cardigan, a patterned shirt collated from old lumberjack shirts and red jeans so tight he can barely move his legs. He has a mini bobble hat on each finger, a tattoo of Sir Michael Parkinson on his left forearm and a green visor on his head. I guess he's running an errand for a studio that makes films for an underground art gallery that no one has heard of. Literally.

That kid. He is ultra flip-out trendy. Max-ultra-bosh. By the time he comes back an hour later, he is no longer fashion forward. Things have moved on. Jeans are baggy now and dark green or mottled pigeon, certainly not red. Shirts are stiff and have Edwardian wing collars. And green visors are a joke. A total macked-out joke.

And the kid? He knows it. The second he walks back in the bar, he cries and runs out. That's how tough things are at the cutting trend-edge.

And that was the kind of bar that hi-lo and LA Dave walk into 17 minutes and 48 seconds later. I time it. With a replica original Casio calculator watch I wore specially for the occasion. I could never have realised how useful it would be. Neither could hi-lo and LA Dave.

Oh, them: hi-lo and LA Dave.

They walk into the bar and everyone stops. They aren't being trendy. They aren't being cool, bosh, ultra-bosh, anti-mack or whatever you want to call it. They are well above that. They are beyond that.

She, hi-lo, wears a dress made out of fourteen old doilies, slung over a white and gold catsuit, with killer heels and a haircut to match. He, LA Dave, wears a pair of white trainers, a Fruit of the Loom t-shirt and George at Asda jeans. I can't tell who looks more midget-gem-macked-out-ultra-bosh. Neither. It isn't a contest.

They see me and then pretend they haven't seen me. I'm used to that. It's part of the ritual. They didn't do it when we met in the office, but then there was no one to do it for. Apart from me. But I didn't count then, and I'm certainly not about to start counting now.

Eventually, they come over and slide onto the two stools I saved for them by the bar.

Can I get them a drink?

– Sure, LA Dave says, flicking a tiny badge adorned with the face of Nicholas Parsons onto the bar. Make mine a Kaliber.

And hi-lo? What will she have?

– Oh, a Babycham.

She sighs and looks out of the window. There is a pigeon, pecking in the dust.

– That pigeon… she says, her voice trailing into distance.

I know what she means.

But we aren't here to talk about pigeons, or any other kind of bird. We are here to talk about 'that' period in the life of the electro-smash-bubble-pop-sensation that was, and still is, Electric Love; 'that' period that no one talks about but everyone wants to know about.

After the triumphs of their first album, 'Can I Have That (Please?)', and the resulting sell-out European tour, the world seemed at their feet and practically every teenager on the planet wanted a piece of them. But then things got difficult for the duo.

LA Dave runs his hands through his hair.

– Yeah, things got totally macked out.

– hi-lo: Yeah. Macked.

– LA Dave: We didn't know what to do. We got totally scared, I guess. After the first album we thought that, like, we couldn't do anything wrong. Like everything we did would be total bosh.

hi-lo drains her glass and orders another drink. She looks at me. Then she looks at LA Dave. And then she looks back at me.

– hi-lo: What I don't get, like, even now, is, like, what actually went wrong? I mean, we totally did the same things, right? We used the same processes that had worked before. We, like, even wore the same clothes and drunk the same drinks. From the same cups. But nothing we did went right. It was all mack.

– LA Dave: Right. For 'Can I…' I had, like, this process that I called 'vintage jam'. Basically, we could use only secondary samples, ones that had been used before. And we decided we should only do cover versions of covers. In other words, all our music should be second-hand, hand-me-down, vintage. Nothing should be new, new. It should all be an interpretation of interpretation. It was about making the unoriginal original. You get me?

– hi-lo: yeah?

I nod, slowly, and then vigorously.

– LA Dave: Well, for this album, right? The second one? You know? 'Plastic Heartbreak'? We did the same thing. But nothing happened. It all just sounded mack.

– hi-lo: Totally.

But the album was still a hit, I insist. The three singles – 'An Eclectic Kettle (Makes Eclectic Tea)', 'Sweep My Path (I'll Get You A Broom)' and the Beatles-inspired mash-up 'Across the Universe (On A Plastic Love Rocket)' – were all mega-dancefloor-smashes.

– Yeah, they both say.

– LA Dave: The album did well, yeah. But, for me, and for hi-lo, it wasn't quite the same. Things weren't quite clicking. I think that sowed the seed for the problems we had with the third album.

hi-lo: We were so macked out by everything that we couldn't even, like, tour.

LA Dave looks at me, and then out of the window. His sunglasses slide down his nose. I can see something glistening in the corner of his eye. I think it's a tear, but then I wonder. I never did find out what that was.

It's another three months before I see hi-lo and LA Dave – the two halves of the electro-bubble-smash-pop-sensation Electric Love – again. Much has happened, both for them and for me.

Me, I'm riding in a parked taxi halfway down the Old Kent Road. It's four in the afternoon on an overcast

September morning in late June. I am not sure what, or who, will greet me in the Wazz Bar, an achingly trendy joint off the Elephant and Castle roundabout.

I've heard rumours. We all have. Rumours that hi-lo has eloped with a Perl programmer from Watford. That LA Dave has opened a sweetshop in Croydon. Suffice to say that, at the time of writing, neither the Perl programmer nor the sweetshop are available for comment, if they ever were.

So, it's with a certain sense of trepidation that I walk into the Wazz Bar. I am five minutes late. Normally, I would be at least 45 minutes early, to soak up the atmosphere and to watch 'them' walk in the door. hi-lo and LA Dave, that is, Electric Love to you and me.

I order a drink—I don't care what—and grab a seat at a table by the bar. I face the door and wait. They, hi-lo and LA Dave, are even later. So, once I have taken a sip of my Blue Nun spritzer, I take in the other customers.

It doesn't take long. Aside from a small man in a large coat and even larger hat nursing a drink at the far end of the bar, and a young boy in high-waisted trousers, Take That cravat, ring master's tailcoat and bright red trilby sitting by the door, the bar is empty. It's hardly a surprise.

Last week, it was reviewed by *Mind Bender* magazine. They told readers they couldn't go. Unless they knew for sure that they were super-bosh-max-flip-out trendy. Not many people have that sort of confidence. Hardly anyone has. Apart from hi-lo and LA Dave, of course.

Fifteen minutes and forty-seven seconds later, they walk in. It's like a nuclear fashion bomb went off in the room. We, all of us, maybe even the stuffed canary behind the bar, look up, amazed. She, hi-lo, is wearing electric green skin-tight trousers, a low-cut frilly long-sleeve white blouse and a luminous yellow scarf around her head, tied like Hilda Ogden. Her bleach-blond hair sticks out at the sides. Her shocking red lipstick glistens in the low lighting. She has a six-inch red stiletto on one foot and a flat, grey Converse on the other. She looks almost majestic as she hobbles over to the bar, fifty bangles on each arm clinking with every disjointed, uncomfortable step. He, LA Dave, is wearing tight tennis shorts, a Blue Harbour fleece from M&S and a pair of beige Hush Puppies. And no socks. She has never looked better. He has never looked worse. Bosh-max-flip-out. Need I say more?

Nine minutes and twelve seconds later, they acknowledge me. hi-lo stares right at me. No expression on her face. She is devastatingly beautiful. And then she looks out of the window.

– Yeah, she whispers.

I know what she means.

A rubbish truck drives past.

– Rubbish, she mouths, her shocking red lipstick glistening with every move of her lips.

But we aren't here to talk about rubbish. We are here to talk about their – Electric Love's – third album. Those are two very different things. Very.

– I ask: So, tell me what happened with the third album?

LA Dave glances across at hi-lo. She looks away. He looks back at me.

– LA Dave: Well, you know what, like, happened. It was totally mack. Everyone hated it, even us.

– hi-lo: Even us.

– LA Dave: Everything about doing the album was totally hard. Mack hard. Nothing was bosh easy. Not one thing.

– Me: Didn't you even have to abandon your world tour as a result?

– LA Dave: Yeah, totally. It was our big chance, to max-out on our success. But it all went south. Didn't it, h?

– hi-lo: Yeah, and we started running into problems in

our personal lives. LA got addicted to antacids after a mild bout of indigestion, and I had a nervous breakdown.

– Why, I ask.

– I think I must have been nervous.

She looks at the table and pushes her chair back. They both do. It's like they need some space between them and the table. Like it's reminding them of something. I ask them what's wrong.

– hi-lo: There was a table then too.

– LA Dave: You know, we tried, like, all sorts of things. We experimented with different genres. I mean, we had to abandon an entire album of Andalusian nose flute music that we spent six months working on. After that, I moved to a commune outside Reading. I thought I would find myself, reach a deeper level of understanding of myself and the universe, which would lift my conscience to a new level and illuminate the artist within.

– Did you, I ask.

– No.

– hi-lo: You did get crabs, though. Didn't you? When you slept with that ugly tart from Newport.

– LA Dave: I thought we said we wouldn't talk about that.

– hi-lo: Yeah? Well, I'm talking about it.

hi-lo looks at me, outraged.

– She was fat, man. And she had a piggy nose, and horrible hair. She was totally ugly. And she was short. Like a midget.

– LA Dave: All right, all right. She was a lovely person.

LA Dave glances at me for support. I smile noncommittally.

– A lovely person, hi-lo asks, mockingly. Is that all?

– LA Dave: And she made great cakes.

– hi-lo: Cakes? Cakes? You could have eaten her cakes without fucking her.

LA Dave looks sheepish. He fiddles with the zip on his Blue Harbour fleece. hi-lo looks angry. She picks at a seam on her electric green trousers. They glare in opposite directions. I wonder what to say.

But then I realise what I should say. After all, I always know what to say. That's the kind of guy I am.

– So, what's the future for Electric Love?

LA Dave brightens up.

– Well, we've just announced some brand new tour dates, and we have booked some time in the studio next week to record new material we've been working on.

– hi-lo: Yeah, and I've been, like, working on some lyrics on my own. Three songs, as a matter of fact. They're called: 'Welsh Tart', 'Lovely Personality (But Have You Seen Her Cellulite?)', and 'Crab-Out'. It's all drawn from personal experience.

hi-lo stares at LA Dave and pulls a string of chewing gum out of her mouth while she arches an eyebrow. LA Dave looks down and tugs at the zip of his fleece again. Then he looks out of the window.

I can see a neon sign reflected in the curve of his lenses. It flashes: Full English Breakfast. It's too late for breakfast. Far too late. LA Dave knows it, hi-lo knows it, I know it. But there is always lunch. It's not too late for that. Lunch is a meal. It's not the same meal—it could never be that—but it's a meal nonetheless. I guess that, sometimes, you just have to make do with what you've got.

POSTSCRIPT

After completing my series of interviews with the ultra-bosh, flip-out duo hi-lo and LA Dave, who form the electro-smash-bubble-pop-sensation Electric Love, things went a bit quiet. To be honest, after the tension they showed when we met in the Wazz Bar in south London, I thought that their insistence that they would go back to the studio to record a fourth album would amount to nothing.

Zero. Zilch. Nada. Less than nothing. An inverse of nothing. A sort of negative creativity void into which their first three albums would be sucked and disappear forever. Maybe taking them with it. That sort of nothing.

But it was not to be.

First, a teenager in low-rise pink trousers and a vermillion shirt, with fifteen gold necklaces tied around his waist and a stuffed pigeon in his back pocket, appeared in my office. He was so flip-out trend-edge that neither of us could speak.

Saying nothing, he handed me a C90 cassette tape that contained the address of a secret website that gave directions to a locked box in a student bedsit in Stanmore, which yielded up nothing less than a demo CD of Electric Love's new album.

Of course, I'm sworn to secrecy, but that won't stop me telling you that it is full of possibly the most exciting dance-floor mash-up bosh-out shoe tunes that I have ever heard. And some of the greasiest chords that have ever been flicked.

If that wasn't enough, then something majestic happened. Last week, in the dead of night at around four in the afternoon, I received an email. It was a fake email from Barclays. I don't even have an account with them. How annoying is that?

However, two minutes later, I got another email. From LA Dave, the man himself, and co-signed hi-lo. I was staggered. So staggered that I'm going to reproduce it for you verbatim.

Hey, it's LA Dave and hi-lo! Yeah, that's right, Electric Love!

You know, we were sitting in the studio just now, and we were, like, totally thinking.

We are working hard on this new album, right? And we're sure it's going to be so anti-mack that it could cause the fall of governments. All over the world.

Well, this morning, we finished mixing three flip-out ultra-bosh tracks that will make your ears melt. Literally.

So while you wait to hear them, we thought we'd send you the titles to get you in the mood: Drop Your Panties (It's A Stick Up)', 'Pass Your Cup (I'll Make Us Some Tea)', and 'That Pain In My Heart (It's Angina)'.

See what I mean? Total maggot!

Love, hi-lo and LA Dave

BLACKS AND WHITES

I forgot to tell you. Last week I saw a woman when I was queuing in the post office. I'm not sure why I was there, I don't think I was posting anything.

Anyway, the woman, she had Tourette's syndrome. She didn't swear or anything like that. She just became extremely frustrated with herself. She screamed and shouted, but tried so hard to contain herself that the screams and shouts came out as yelps and barks, like a pained dog.

I was sorry for her. She was aged around forty-five and trendily dressed in a padded black coat. She seemed success-ful, confident almost, in her own way. But her face was pale white, tired and haunted. She caught no one's eye, and her body was tense, as if ready to spring. She must have been living with her condition all her life, containing it, explaining it, dreading it. She must be so tired of her barks and yelps.

Others in the queue were less sympathetic. A black man and a white woman, both middle-aged, sniggered and rolled their eyes at her outbursts. It made me angry and I wanted to say something. But I didn't. The woman was clearly capable of looking after herself and I wouldn't have wanted to patronise her. She'd probably had enough of that.

At one point, I became distracted by my own thoughts. And then a position at a counter became free and, when I looked up, she had gone. The black man and white woman still talked, but no longer about her. They had been brought together by their prejudice. They were conjoined in shamefulness.

I thought about all of this today, while I was out running. As the woman, her dark hair, quivering voice and padded overcoat, returned to my mind, I passed branches, decomposed leaves, churned earth and yellow, matted grass. I don't know why I thought of her. Maybe I was simply turning over recent events, as if in a dream.

As I ran on, I saw a long, deep puddle that reflected perfectly the white clouds overhead. And all around it were rooks, heavy and silent, occasionally dipping their beaks into the water.

They watched me pass, and I saw the ready spring in their legs and the slight opening of their wings, just in case I should step over. I wished I could have reassured them, told them that I would never do them any harm. But how could I convince them that I wasn't like all the rest?

So I ran on, with only the memory of the suspicion in their eyes.

THE HILL

Today, on the hill,
you shook,
I froze.
Hours later, I cried.

ON MY WAY HOME

ON THE TUBE, SHE, GLOWING WITH A DRUNKEN SHEEN, GAZED at him and flushed.

She stepped forward to be with him but recoiled as her hair was thrown awry by the dusty metallic breeze blowing hard through the open window between the carriages.

– Come here, she mouthed pleadingly.

He shook his head, folded his arms and stared at the other passengers. His cufflinks glinted in the neon light.

His small beard was untidy. He was also drunk. Undone. Ragged.

She smoothed her black dress repeatedly.

I looked away, and caught the eye of another couple sitting opposite and wondered about their life. Were they rich? Were they heading back to a town villa with bare floor-boards and expensive wine? Her dress was vintage crêpe de Chine, his suit was well cut and expensive. They talked in hushed tones, smiling occasionally, conspiratorially. There was a line of grey in her hair that disappeared as she self-consciously pushed it back into her dark curls.

I turned back to the drunk couple. He smiled at her and crossed the divide. They embraced and kissed.

He had lost his point but, then, I think he always knew he would.

SLEEP

It catches you unawares. The smothering embrace, reaching around you, collecting you in its arms, covering you, brushing your eyes. Shut.

Not always delicately. Occasionally forcefully. Rarely can you resist.

The rocking of a train carriage. The quiet of a darkened room. The artificial glare of an airport. The stultification of a meeting. The metronomic words of a book. The heat of an unfamiliar climate.

Today, it is urgent, the call of sleep. I sense its soft tendrils around my eyes. It lies heavy on my chest. My arms are glutinous. The skin on my calves crawls.

When I am like this, no stimulant will ameliorate, no brightness will pierce, no sound will penetrate.

I am warm yet cold. Heavy yet floating. I cannot climb. Out.

ABOUT THE AUTHOR

L.A. Davenport is an Anglo-Irish author and journalist. He has been writing stories, and more, since he was a wee bairn, as his grandpa used to say. Among other things, he likes long walks, typewriters and big cups of tea.

To find out when L.A. Davenport has a new book out, and get the latest updates, visit his official website at Pushing the Wave.

PRAISE FOR L.A. DAVENPORT

[*The Nucleus of Reality* is] a beautifully described story of a man trying to remember why he ended up losing everything but himself.

— EMILY QUINN

[It] is strange, existential, and curious. It might give you a lot to ponder about if you dig deep enough... [It's] a stream of consciousness first-person novel with the most unreliable narrator you've ever met.

— RUMMY'S RECS

Trust me, you're in for a mind-bending ride...I had no idea how it would end.

— KAM BROOK

[*My Life is a Dog*] is a quick read, it's a sweet read, it's exactly the kind of thing to buoy your spirits after a long week (or 2020). I do recommend this for you or the dog lover in your life.

— THE IRRESPONSIBLE READER

There is only one word that could describe this book and that is adorable...I really adored this wee book and I adored Kevin and it's clear his owner also does! Such a sweet book.

— BOOKS BY BINDU

Readers [of *Escape*] will eagerly follow John's character arc from a self-destructive, grieving widower to an individual fighting to clear his name and take down a criminal organization.

— THE BOOKLIFE PRIZE

I wanted to know more, to see where the little strings led and ultimately see who was trying to *Escape*.

— PERRY WOLFECASTLE

If you're after a bit of a thriller combined with romantic suspense, then *Escape* is definitely one to add to your (probably ever growing) TBR list . . . I didn't want to put it down!

— EMILY QUINN

BY L.A. DAVENPORT

FICTION

The Nucleus of Reality, or the Recollections of Thomas P—

Escape

No Way Home

Dear Lucifer and Other Stories

The Marching Band Emporium

NON-FICTION

My Life as a Dog

More Life as a Dog

Printed in Great Britain
by Amazon